For my family

First published 2016 by Walker Books Ltd, 87 Vauxhall Walk, London SE11 5HJ

1 3 5 7 9 10 8 6 4 2

Copyright © 2016 Neal Layton

The right of Neal Layton to be identified as author/illustrator of this work has been asserted by him in accordance with the Copyright, Designs and Patents Act 1988

This book has been typeset in Fell Type Roman

Printed in China

British Library Cataloguing in Publication Data:
a catalogue record for this book is available from the British Library

ISBN 978-1-4063-5821-6

www.walker.co.uk

the tree

neal layton

WALKER BOOKS
AND SUBSIDIARIES
LONDON · BOSTON · SYDNEY · AUCKLAND

A tree,

a nest,

a drey,
a hollow

and a
burrow.

The new arrivals,

the
wonderful
plan,

the hard work

and the
terrible
surprise.

The broken nest.

Back to work:
measuring, lifting,

hammering
and painting.

A better
burrow,
a cosier
hollow,

a sturdier drey,
a mended nest,
and a ...

— happy —
home.